SCM
Schneider, Antonie
You Shall Be King!

Copyright © 1995 by Nord-Süd Verlag AG, Gossau Zürich, Switzerland
First published in Switzerland under the title *Ich bin der kleine König*.
English translation copyright © 1995 by North-South Books Inc.

First published in the United States, Great Britain, Canada,
Australia, and New Zealand in 1995 by North-South Books,
an imprint of Nord-Süd Verlag AG, Gossau Zürich, Switzerland.

Distributed in the United States by North-South Books Inc., New York.

Library of Congress Cataloging-in-Publication Data is available.
A CIP catalogue record for this book is available from The British Library.

ISBN 1-55858-385-8 (trade binding)
1 3 5 7 9 TB 10 8 6 4 2
ISBN 1-55858-386-6 (library binding)
1 3 5 7 9 LB 10 8 6 4 2

Printed in Belgium

You Shall Be King!

By Antonie Schneider
Illustrated by Christa Unzner

Translated by J. Alison James

North-South Books / New York / London

One morning, when the sun was shining and Grandfather had gone for a walk in the forest, there came a knock on the window.

The boy looked out and saw a girl waving to him from behind the apple tree. When he opened the door, she stood there, laughing.

"Come out and play!" she cried. "You shall be king and I'll be the queen. Of course we'll need a sorcerer, too."

The girl opened her bag and pulled out a shining cloth, a golden crown, and a small chest.

"What's in the chest?" asked the boy.

"You'll see soon enough," said the girl. "Now all you need is a throne. Do you have one in the house?"

The boy hesitated. Then he went inside and came back with Grandfather's big chair.

"Please be seated, Your Highness," said the girl, as she dropped the cloth around his shoulders.

The dog barked and the hens cackled as they watched through the fence. "You can play too!" said the girl to the animals. "The king will need loyal subjects.

"And now," said the girl, slowly opening the chest. "Now you receive the golden ring. Now you are truly king!"

The loyal subjects gathered around the throne. The girl pulled a
well-worn book from her bag. "It is time to begin the story," she
announced. "Everyone has a part."

Slowly, dramatically, she began.

"Once in this green meadow there was a kingdom. And in this kingdom there lived a handsome king. Everything in the kingdom belonged to him: the blackbird and her eggs, the hunting dog, the sun, the forest, the icy sea, and the fire-spewing mountain. Even the mosquitoes and elephants, robbers and saints, chocolate and gold, mailboxes and motorcycles, daisies and ship captains and puppets and police, were his. The only thing he didn't have was a queen. . . ."

"What do I need a queen for?" asked the boy, who was getting bored and tired of sitting still.

"Watch out!" cried the girl as she pulled a red mask over her face. Now she was a sorcerer.

"I have come for the ring," said the sorcerer. "It holds the key to a secret treasure. Lend it to me, and I will return it along with fabulous riches."

The sorcerer begged and pleaded and cried so imploringly that the king finally agreed.

"Ha! I tricked you!" cried the sorcerer, and threw the ring over the hedge into the brook.

Shocked, the boy fell from the throne.

"Without your ring, you are not king!" said the sorcerer.
"Now you must wander the wide world."

"I don't want to be king anyway," said the boy as he wandered through the garden gate. "I'm tired of this game. It's boring." And he stuffed the crown in his pocket.

But the girl came after him. "You must find work!" she cried. "Knock on that stone over there. That is the castle."

The boy gave a reluctant tap on the stone.

The castle answered, "If you're looking for work, you may stay here and be the cook."

The girl pointed to the sandbox. That was the kitchen. The boy sat in the sandbox and made dandelion soup and sand cakes.

The girl wrapped herself in a golden cloth and put a crown on her head and a ring of flowers in her hair. "I'm a princess," she said. "And these are the most delicious sand cakes I've ever tasted."

The cook was pleased. While they were eating, the cook and the princess found many things to laugh and talk about.

"You know," said the cook. "I'm really a king. I've just lost my ring."

"Then we must find it!" exclaimed the princess happily. "Hurry, we will take the coach through the castle gates."

Just then Grandfather came back from the woods. "What's going on here?" he asked.

"Out of my way, good sir!" called the cook. "We are off on a quest for the ring!"

"Good luck to you then," said Grandfather.

Once outside the castle, the cook turned to the princess. "If we can find the ring," he said, "and I become king, then you could be a queen instead of just a princess."

"Wait here!" said the princess. She ran to the water barrel behind the hedge and came back carrying a wide leaf. "I bring you a fish from the sea," she declared.

The cook split open the fish. Inside lay the king's golden ring.

Then the cook became king again and he took his new queen by the hand. Together they ran to Grandfather. "Grandfather, look, I am king and she is my queen, and the meadow is our kingdom and the big stone is the castle, the sandbox is the kitchen, and your chair is the throne."

"Well, well," said Grandfather. "Then I suppose I am the cook.
I'll go and warm the soup. It's time for lunch."

"Lunchtime!" cried the girl. "I have to get home!"

As she ran through the gate, she called back, "Tomorrow we'll slay the dragon, the scourge of the kingdom."

"I'll polish my sword tonight," answered the boy. "Don't worry, I'll be ready!"